Me & Mama

COZBI A. CABRERA

A DENENE MILLNER BOOK
SIMON & SCHUSTER BOOKS FOR YOUNG READERS
NEW YORK   LONDON   TORONTO   SYDNEY   NEW DELHI

**Good morning
to you,**

sings Mama, bright as sun.
Sometimes she sings it like the
birthday song.

I've tiptoed to where she
is in the house.
It smells like cinnamon.
Papa and Luca are still sleeping,
but I want to
be everywhere Mama is.

I put my nose to the window.
My breath makes a cloud inside.
The clouds outside are wearing shadows.
The wind is painting the outside window
with beads of water.

It's raining! I say.
The perfect day for boots
and puddles, says Mama.
Bathroom first, she says.
Then water! I say.

This is Mama's cup.
Sometimes I take a cool sip,
but I have to be careful
because her cup is breakable.

This is my cup.

Mama's cup goes *clink, clink*
with a spoon.
My cup goes *duh, duh*.

Clink, clink, clink!
Duh, duh.
Clink, clink, clink, clink, clink!

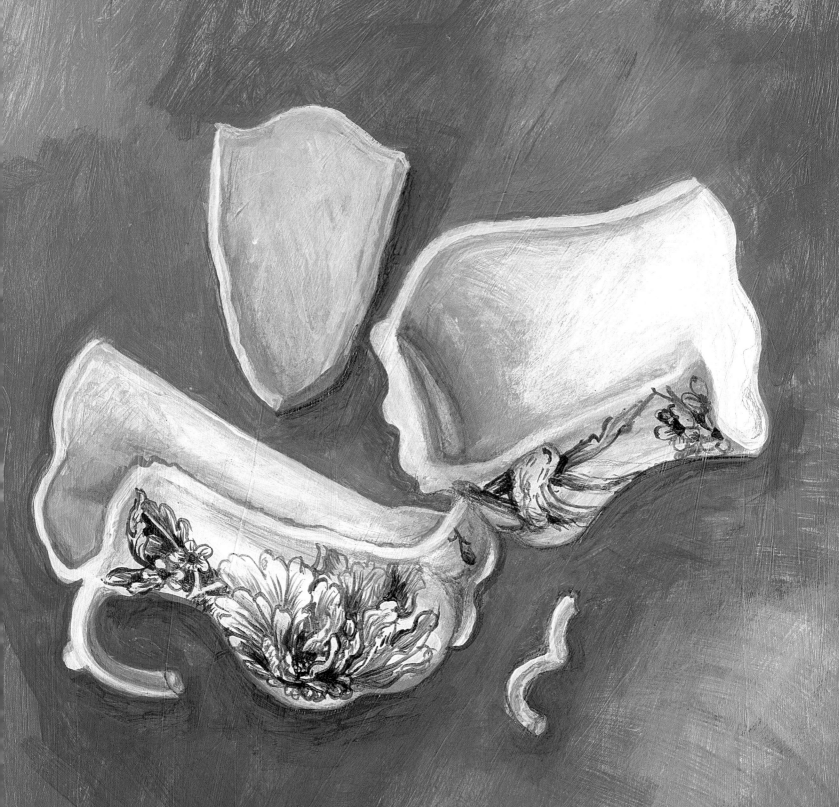

Sometimes things break, Mama says.

This is Mama's toothbrush.

This is mine.
I get less toothpaste.

*Round my teeth with
little circles, Mama says.
Round my teeth with
little circles, I say.*

It's shower
and dress time.
Mama holds
up my towel.
A shower is
warm rain that
gets you going.

Mama and I both have
silver dresses.
I wear mine with
silver shoes.
They're my favorite.

*Today is not our silver
dress day,* Mama tells me.
I put my silver dress back
on the hanger and pick
the plaid pants instead.

Comb hair, says Mama.
She points to my chair.
I'm hungry, I say.
Mama's thought of this ahead of time.
She has warm oatmeal in the pot.

This is Mama's bowl.
She likes berries.

This is my bowl.
I like bananas.

Comb hair, Mama says again.
I don't want the bumblebee barrette.
I don't like the bumblebee barrette, I say.
Mama closes her hand.
She knows I mean just today.
She gives me the blue barrette.
Comb hair, I say.

I point to Mama's chair.
Mama smiles.
I give Mama the purply
pink barrette.
It matches her dress.
She calls it fuchsia.

Out we go! I say.
Max is waiting.
These are my rain boots
and those are Mama's.
Mama's rain boots are
bigger than mine.
And they're red.

I watch for Max's tail
before I close the door.
Max doesn't wear boots.

Outside a pecker pecks.
The sidewalk is longer than it is wide.
I love the grass that grows in the in-between.
It's moss, Mama says.
It's velvet, I say.

A hole is where a branch was.
Nests are left behind in winter.
Some things don't let go. But for what?
The stores are boxes filled with people.

We sing out loud to sky. Sky is taller,
taller than the trees.
Mama says a song is highs and lows.

SPLASH!

The outside clouds are pink with
a sleepy sun.
The day and our good are done.

Mama puts me and Luca to bed.
Our day is done earlier than
Mama and Papa's.
It's just that way when you're
growing.

Mama reads to us.
I read to Mama.
I begin each story with *Sometimes*.
Mama laughs. She throws her head back
and shines her teeth.
I laugh too.

You're my best girl, Mama whispers.
Luca is already asleep.
I slip through the blanket tunnel
she closes by my chin.

There's the kiss.
I love you, Mama! I yell.

She turns off the light.

My mouth gets sleepy first.
The walls are dark except by
the window, where the stars
are hanging.
I close my eyes and let the
day spin me some pictures.

There's Max and Luca and Papa and
Mama's laugh and tree holes and tall
songs and mossy velvet as green as grass
and full boxes and a blue barrette and
a whole cup and a beaded window and
warm indoor rain.

Oh and oh . . .

There'll be me and Mama.

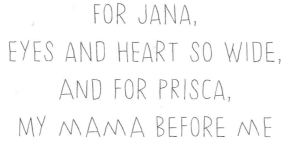

FOR JANA,
EYES AND HEART SO WIDE,
AND FOR PRISCA,
MY MAMA BEFORE ME

SIMON & SCHUSTER BOOKS FOR YOUNG READERS
An imprint of Simon & Schuster Children's Publishing Division
1230 Avenue of the Americas, New York, New York 10020
Copyright © 2020 by Cozbi A. Cabrera
SIMON & SCHUSTER BOOKS FOR YOUNG READERS is a trademark of Simon & Schuster, Inc.
For information about special discounts for bulk purchases, please contact
Simon & Schuster Special Sales at 1-866-506-1949 or business@simonandschuster.com.
The Simon & Schuster Speakers Bureau can bring authors to your live event.
For more information or to book an event, contact the Simon & Schuster Speakers Bureau
at 1-866-248-3049 or visit our website at www.simonspeakers.com.
Book design by Lizzy Bromley • The text for this book was set in Fairfield.
The illustrations for this book were rendered in acrylics.
0221 LAK
4 6 8 10 9 7 5
Library of Congress Cataloging-in-Publication Data
Names: Cabrera, Cozbi A., author, illustrator.
Title: Me & Mama / Cozbi A. Cabrera.
Description: First edition. | New York : Denene Millner Books, [2020] |
Summary: For a little girl on a rainy day, the best place to be is with Mama.
Identifiers: LCCN 2019010816 (print) | LCCN 2019014571 (eBook)
ISBN 9781534454217 (hardcover) | ISBN 9781534454224 (eBook)
Subjects: | CYAC: Mothers and daughters—Fiction.
Classification: LCC PZ7.1.C13 (eBook) | LCC PZ7.1.C13 Me 2020 (print) | DDC [E]—dc23
LC record available at https://lccn.loc.gov/2019010816